MW00327159

As a child, Juju's family took turns making up bedtime stories and songs. Those moments were filled with delight, but more importantly, it was time spent with her siblings and parents. Juju was known for her wit, sarcasm, and storytelling. She began to embellish the characters and plots, telling the stories across the age spectrum. Those years, Juju wrote as a hobby and presented many stories to friends and families as reading gifts. She does want to warn the faint of heart – don't read these alone at night.

I would like to shout a big thank you to Steve, Grant, Melissa, Becca, Chance, Brenda, Mac, and Momma C for encouraging me and listening to my stories and rewrites over the past few months. I might have been a bit annoying, just a bit.

Juju

THE COSTLY WISH

AUSTIN MACAULEY PUBLISHERS™

LONDON · CAMBRIDGE · NEW YORK · SHARJAH

Ordering Information:
Quantity sales: special discounts are available on quantity purchases by corporations, associations, and others. For details, contact the publisher at the address below.

Publisher's Cataloging-in-Publication data
Juju
The Costly Wish

ISBN 9781647503307 (Paperback)
ISBN 9781647503291 (Hardback)
ISBN 9781647503314 (ePub e-book)

Library of Congress Control Number: 2020918712

www.austinmacauley.com/us

First Published (2020)
Austin Macauley Publishers LLC
40 Wall Street, 28th Floor
New York, NY 10005
USA

mail-usa@austinmacauley.com
+1 (646) 5125767

I tell you this story to warn you. You need to be careful. Not too many years ago, I was 12, when I learned a very valuable lesson. It was fall, and the air was crisp and breezy. Not unusual for this time of year. A carnival passed through the sleepy-eyed town of Oxford. Like most small southern establishments, it was built mostly of wood materials. It was the sort of town that lent itself to fresh air and plenty of room to run and experience life. The center of town had a square encircled with local shops and cafes. On Sundays, at noon and 6 pm, one would hear the gentle harmony of the church bells as they walked the paved sidewalks past the red maples and majestic golden ginkgo trees. The stores' windows displayed their best wares and sales. It was a small town of regulars and good ole boys. Everyone was looking forward to the rides and fun to offset the reoccurring high school football games.

The large caravan set up their bulky blue and white tents and rusty rides on the far end of town butting up to a thick wilderness and a small potter's field. At night, the strung lights from the carnival lit up the whole sky. Smoke from the food trucks would bellow and churn out more and more. The requests for funnel cakes, burgers, and fries were never-ending. Children and their parents were delighted at the spectacular events of sights and games. There were dancing bears and playful monkeys in the cages to watch and stare. The chained elephants would blow their trumpets, circling their trainer with the long whip, and the lions perched on decorative barrels would roar. The crowd cheered at the excitement and noise. Balloons, bright-colored banners, and the smells of popcorn, sweets, and hotdogs filled the air.

In the middle of the carnival was a Conestoga wagon made of faded redwood. The painted images were worn and decayed. The ole mule tied behind the structure appeared half alive, his gray muzzle, protruding ribs and hips, and long teeth foretold a long history of plowing and hard work. A small sign hanging across the porch read "Fortune Teller." It swung in the fall evening winds. At the doorway of the wagon, an old woman sat watching the people walking back and forth between rides. One little boy who had wandered away from his mother approached the old woman. "What are you doing?" asked the little boy.

Looking down from her entryway, she narrowed her eyes, sizing up the little boy. "Come in and see," coaxed the woman. "Come in and see." The woman reached down and pulled the little one up the small rickety steps and into the red wagon, then quickly closed the curtain behind him. The musty smell of dampness, cold, and age permeated the small enclosure. Inside, it was quite dark, so the old woman struck a match and lit a candle on the table. The light flickered and caused the shadows to move about the wagon walls. The little boy became very frightened and could not speak. The old woman peered down at the little boy and then waved her arms over his head and began to chant. He sat very still, frozen with fear, watching with wide blue eyes. Finally, she abruptly stopped and looked into her crystal ball that lay in the middle of her table. "What wish do you want, little boy?" the old woman asked. "What wish do you want?"

At first, the little boy could think of nothing except how frightened he was. But soon, he gained some courage to speak up, "I don't have a wish now; may I have a wish to think about and use later?"

The old woman hesitated for a moment and then responded, "How will you pay me, little boy, for the wish?"

He shook his head, "I don't know, I don't have any money."

She looked at him, disappointed. She too was a sad sight. Lonely and old, she barely made enough to eat and traveled with the carnival because they tolerated her kind. Her family long gone, she had only her red wagon and the crystal ball she used to make up grand stories of fortunes for paying customers. Her hair was completely white and wiry. Her skin was wrinkled and peppered with age. She had lost most of her teeth and her smile over decades of abuse and poverty. "You have nothing?" she asked.

Digging into his blue jean pocket, the little boy pulled out an opened pack of gum. "I have this," he offered.

The old woman just shook her head, "I'm hungry, boy. This just won't do. Get out. Just get out." And, pushing him toward the door, she collapsed on the floor. He turned just in time to see her fall but could not stop the accident from happening. Her small frame hit the corner of the table, knocking the candle and glass ball to the floor, where it shattered into pieces. Her last breath was a sharp gasp and then nothing.

"Mom! Mom!" the boy screamed. He flew out the door and down the steps. "Mom!" His mother came running,

9

grabbed her son up, and held him tight. "Where have you been?"

"Mom, she's hurt!"

Looking directly into his face, "Who is hurt?"

Pointing and half dragging his mother toward the red wagon steps, he said "The old woman!"

By the time the authorities had been called and the crowd dispersed, the ground had frosted over. Standing outside the wagon, the ringmaster of the carnival, still in his long black tails, gave as much information as he could remember about the old woman, which wasn't much. She had no family, no friends, and no money. The town's coroner showed up late with scotch stanched breath, red-nosed and watery-eyed. He lumbered up the stairs of the wagon, grasping tightly to the rail. Inside, the extent of his exam was to lift her hand and feel for a pulse. The local police officer, a four-year veteran of the force, just rolled his eyes and shook his head, dismayed this man still had a job.

A small group of carnivals workers had collected outside the wagon. It had been a long day and there was a chill in the air. They had passed around straws. It was their way of selecting who would be cleaning up. Two of them were handed shovels. They have had this happen before and knew the course that would follow. This town would not take on the responsibility of burying an old woman with no money, family, or friends. No one cared. She would be buried tonight before the ground got colder and harder to dig. Already the two contemplated how deep they would dig before deciding it was enough so animals would not disturb the ground. They chose the spot next to the tree because there was less rock. When they finished the hole, it resembled one more for a child – not big enough for her to be laid out. Two police officers assisted in wrapping up her body in the rug which she had been lying on. The coroner came back from his truck with a roll of duct tape and proceeded to dispense large swaths to wrap around the rug to hold the binding together. They carried her out and down the steps of the wagon. She wasn't heavy.

No words were spoken. No prayer. No goodbyes. With minimal effort, they lowered her body, wrapped in a rug and bound with duct tape, down into the hole. They shoveled and kicked dirt over her frame until the hole was filled. The veteran looked around on the ground for a stone but saw none. Looking back at the wagon, his eye caught sight of the little sign reading 'Fortune Teller', and he ran up the steps and snatched it down. He took it back over to the mound of earth and laid it over her grave. And then, before the glint of the rising sun peered through the pines, they left. All of them. The carnival, the coroner, the police officers, the red wagon, and mule. All gone. A lone empty field with one lone tree and one single freshly earthed mound with a torn down sign laid across its middle.

The little boy returned, alone. In his hands, he held a coffee cup filled with dirt with a small plant unearthed he had found that morning. The humming sound coming from the small figure moving toward the mound was the only song the little boy knew. He repeated it over and over again. He stepped over the debris left from the events of the night prior. Paper cups, cigarette butts, needles, beer cans, and discarded half-eaten food. He stopped at the mound.

Solemnly staring down, the little boy started, "I thought about my wish. I wish I had a friend." But no one heard. No one was around to hear. Sadly, the little boy, much like the old woman, had no friends. Ever. He was lonely and different. He knew he was different. He didn't know why but just knew that he was. He pulled a spoon from his back pocket and began to dig a small circular hole in the middle of the mound. About the size of his hand. He then turned the cup upside down and the plant along with its dirt fell out.

He buried the plant's roots, exposing the small leaves and stem which appeared limp and slumped over. He looked around and saw a beer can. He picked it up and noted it still had some content left which he poured over the plant. Wiping his hands on his pants, he stood up. *There, that ought to do it*, he smiled. From a distance, he heard his mother calling his name. And, with that, he left, humming his song.

Over the course of several weeks complicated with massive rains and thunderstorms, no one had been to the field. No one noticed the change. So you understand how surprised the little boy was when he returned that early spring to discover a garden sanctuary of different shapes and colors. There was an overwhelming array of textures of flowering shrubs, radiant perennials, and an enormous tree with creeping green vines peppered with oversized green leaves hanging from the top branches and kissing the ground.

He was alone of course. He wandered about the beauty of it all, humming his song until he finally reached the tree. It's then, that he took hold of the vine that hung down from the branches, and with a quick skip and hop, he was swinging back and forth, letting the winds flow through his hair; his laughter and outbursts exposed a perfect set of clean white teeth. The tree itself seemed to sway with the child, and the vines wrapped around his warm body, taking him higher and further into its branches as if protecting him from the world below. The tree flourished that summer, and so did the little boy. Every day he would go to the beautiful garden and swing on the vines on the tree. Every day until another found his sanctuary.

He had seen the little boy on several occasions with his mother uptown shopping. He recognized the little boy was different and was a loner. While out, he noted the little boy always stayed near his mother. This morning, out of boredom, he followed the little boy and his mother home.

Once at their home, he found it easy to watch them from their windows, which they never closed. He had done this with other families and had made off with some really cool stuff. They didn't have a dog, so nothing aroused their suspicion. He waited outside picking at a scab on his elbow and smoked a few cigarettes, flicking the butts on the ground where he stood. Near noon, the little boy left the house with a bag and blanket. He never looked back and was unaware of the shadow. Watching this little dude humming and swinging his brown paper bag grabbed the follower's attention. Twice while following, he lost sight of the little boy, but soon caught up, keeping enough distance not to draw attention. He noted the little boy appeared to be heading toward the end of town, where the carnivals like to set up. And just like any other day, the boy humming his song reached his garden and straight toward his tree he went, spreading out a blanket under its shade. He then proceeded to sit down and opened his bag. He had brought a lunch of peanut butter and jelly sandwiches and a green metal thermos of Kool-Aid. He had taken only two bites before he noticed the shadow of the older boy looming over him and it startled him.

"What are you doing, kid?" asked the stranger.

The little boy sensed danger and stood up quickly. "Ah, nothing."

"So what is this place?" he said, surveying the landscape and reaching for the knotty vine. "Do you swing on this?" he queried further. And then gave it a tug.

"Ah, yes, sometimes," the little boy responded nervously, his eyes darting back toward the entrance of the field. The little boy could detect a quiver from the tree as the leaves moved in the silence. It didn't trust the stranger either.

Before the boy could step away, the intrusive stranger jumped up on the vine, pulling hard, snapping some tender branches that fell to the barren ground and wilted before the boy's eyes.

"No, no, no," whimpered the little boy. His pleading and tear-stained face went unnoticed. And suddenly, the whole vine snapped, hurling the insensitive oaf to the ground.

"Whoa!" he sneered and threw what part of the vine remained in his hand to the ground. He turned his focus on the boy, "You knew I could have been hurt!" His anger boiled up so quickly that his vision blurred. And taking the thermos, he began to beat the boy. And he didn't stop beating, not even when the handle came off in his hand, because then, he just used his fists. The sickening thud,

thud, thud, along with his heavy breathing were all the sounds coming from the field.

He sat down, exhausted. He sat there staring at the heap for what felt like a season. He actually lost track of time. He smoked two more cigarettes. In his mind, he ran several scenarios. All of them started with burying the body. Leaning back, he looked around for anything to ease his task. He found nothing, other than the branch he had knocked off earlier. Using the end of the branch, he began digging a hole next to the body. He worked feverously at the dry earth, moving dirt with his bare hands at times. Wiping the sweat off his brow with his arm, he rolled the body into the hole. *Boy, that kid was small,* he made a mental note. He could tell no one. There wasn't anyone to tell – it was not like he had friends.

He finished off the last of the little boy's sandwiches. He gathered the blanket, canister, and handle and shoved those into the grave. And, to mark his accomplishment, he stabbed the limb he had knocked down earlier on top of the new mound. It looked odd with a stick protruding out of the earth. The whole place looked dreary with the stick and slumping tree, weeds, chert-like ground, and leftover debris from past events still covering the field.

"I don't know what this kid found in this place," he muttered. Then turning around, he left. He headed back toward home on the other side of town, taking the back roads and paths so as not to be seen. He took the long-lost culverts of the South railroad trail coming out on Price Street. *Wonder how long it will be before he's reported missing,* he thought. He realized once home that his pants' pockets were empty and sighed out loud, "Damn, I didn't get anything today except this stupid-looking lump." He always liked to grab stuff and sell whatever he could for pot. He loved pot. He loved weed so much, it got him kicked off the football team. Somebody turned him, he didn't know who, but he wanted to. He fell asleep across his bed, waiting.

He heard the front door slam shut; that would be his mother returning from work. From his bed, he sat quietly, listening to her open drawers and clanking dishes. "Dinner!" she screamed from the kitchen. "Dinner!"

He came out of his room and went directly to the kitchen table. Dishes from breakfast and a full saucer of cigarette butts littered the counter. The McDonald's bag lay on the table. "What did you get?" he asked.

She reached back to redo the rubber band holding back her graying thin hair. "What does it matter?" she responded and then added, "It's dinner. Stop that incessant humming."

"I'm not humming," he quipped back. He reached for the bag and emptied the contents on the table. "Did you get ketchup?"

She rolled her eyes in exasperation, ignoring the fries that fell to the floor. "Did you get the laundry done?" she questioned back. She already knew what the answer would be. "Did you get high today?"

She touched the side of her face, still feeling the tenderness on the cheek. She could tell from the reflection in the oven door glass that it was still red – likely a bruise tomorrow. Before he could lie to her, there was a knock at the front door. He shoved a burger in his mouth. She went to the door, peeked through the stained yellow curtain, and then yanked open the door. Standing on the deck surveying

16

the waste that covered the porch and yard was a veteran police officer.

"What do you want?" she said, folding her arms across her chest and leaning back against the door frame. She recognized him from their earlier encounter.

"Good evening, Ma'am," he managed a smile. He had been coached on how to approach and question civilians. "We're in the area, looking for a little boy who has not come home and asking the public to be on the lookout or if they have seen him." He recognized her too and wondered where her son was that he had seen earlier.

Inside still sitting at the table, he stopped chewing, so he could hear the conversation coming from the porch. He wished the kitchen sink would stop dripping as it was drowning out some of the officer's words. *Crap*, he thought. He stood up and moved to the window, back enough not to be seen but close enough to hear; he had waited too long and only caught the last sentence. "He's been missing for several hours and his mother is desperately worried."

A smug smile began to emerge. He thought about going back to that mother's house to grab some stuff. Thinking it through, he decided to wait this out. Everyone will be looking for the boy, so he would just lie low. Without looking back, the veteran walked to his cruiser. The hair on his arm was standing up. He believed in his intuitions. Something was up, but he had no idea what it meant. It was his last stop as his shift was ending. *I sure hope they find this kid*, he thought as he walked away.

A couple of days had passed before he couldn't stand it any longer. He knew he was addicted to pot; if you smoke it every day, you get that way. After a couple of days, your skin crawls and the irritation is undeniable. Which was where he was – miserable. "Stop that damn humming!" his mother yelled again. At that point, she just threw him out of the house. "Just get out!"

And that's how he ended up standing at the entrance of the field perplexed at its change. It was a garden sanctuary of different shapes, colors, and textures of flowering shrubs, radiant perennials, and two enormous trees with creeping green vines peppering with oversized green leaves hanging from the top branches and kissing the ground. "Am I high?" he queried.

He found himself beneath the trees, looking up into its branches and seeing nothing but green lush leaves beckoning him to reach out and grab hold, which is what he did. With a lofty leap, he took hold of the vines, swinging back and forth, so unaware of the vines wrapping around his feet, and then his hands. He was being pulled higher into the branches. A distant hum from above drew his attention, which caused him to look up. That's when one of the vines completely circled his neck and started to draw in. He felt the vines tightening and he began to struggle, all the while the humming becoming louder, drowning out his thrashing and his efforts to tear at the vines. He waited too late to scream for help. The leaves covered over his face, muffling his cries. Soon, the writhing stopped.

On a hunch, the veteran arrived at the edge of the field, barren and littered with debris; he surveyed the area. Nothing but two large trees, which appeared to be catching the wind from a slow-moving storm coming from the west, were the only living things this field yielded. Several times, he turned, hearing what he thought sounded like a hum, but realized it was likely the weather changing. It wasn't too long after the boys went missing that the carnival stopped coming to town. No one ventured out that way anymore.

The Moss

The rays from the late evening sun began to filter through the tall pines behind Kelly and Amber's new backyard. Shade from the pines and oaks sucked up every drop of the soil's moisture, leaving tree roots exposed and bare spots across the yard. Having arrived five weeks ago, Kelly and Amber were without friends. The emptied cardboard boxes, used earlier as docking stations for spaceships, lined the porch. There were still boxes to unpack in the garage, but their father had had to go to work, so things were getting unpacked slowly. A narrow trail leading away from the screened backdoor out to the sidewalk allowed their mother to occasionally step out and check on the girls.

The aroma from the dinner cooking in the kitchen drifted through the screen porch. Their mother was such a great cook and every meal was something to look forward to. She used secret recipes from her mother. She always cooked their favorites but warned them that when she was growing up, she had to eat all her vegetables. She hated okra and Brussels sprouts. She would recant how her sister and brother would try to hide the foods they didn't like in their napkins. Her children would laugh at the stories.

Tonight was chicken. Having tried earlier to raid the kitchen cabinets for snacks and having been chased out of the kitchen, the two girls were getting very hungry. To occupy their time before dinner, Kelly and Amber now focused on angling the magnifying glass on the busy ants below. With slumped heads slightly touching and in deep concentration, they tried with difficulty to catch the fading rays of the evening sun. The ants scurried along without worry.

Dressed in matching tunic tops, the girls from a distance appeared as twins. However, Kelly, one year older, differed from Amber. Kelly's eyes were mischievously dark brown and it was often her inquisitive nature that got her in trouble. Amber had a fairer complexion. Amber often received the same punishment for faithfully following her older sister's lead. So it was not surprising that when Kelly decided to leave the yard, Amber would follow obediently and without question.

"No," said Kelly, "she said no."

Amber looked up. "But why?" she asked. Kelly shrugged her shoulders and decidedly plopped down beside her sister. The girls from outside the house heard the telephone. It was answered before the second ring. Kelly knew her mother, anxious to hear from their father, would be on the phone for a while. The two sat there in silence, watching the ants.

After several minutes, Kelly leaned back and looked into the sky. "I figure," she said with a smile, "if we left now, we'd be back before she even knew we had gone. Supper won't be ready for at least another hour and she's on the phone talking with Dad."

"What time does your watch say?" asked Amber.

Shaking her wrist, "I don't know, it's not working again," responded Kelly with a frown. "Well, if we can just get back before six, we should be good." With heads cocked to one side, both waited until they heard their mother's burst of laughter, followed by a cascade of giggles before they set off across the street.

Kelly whispered to Amber, "Only if you double dog dare me." Without another second wasted, the two left in a half-run down the sidewalk. They paused only to let a car pass at the street corner. It sped so fast, that the wheels screeched as it took the corner. The man and woman in the car looked startled to see the children. "That was weird," Kelly stated. "Wonder where they're going in such a hurry?"

From a distance, their brightly covered outfits meshed. As they ran on, the two brown-headed children were indistinguishable. By the time they reached the barbed wire fence, the sun had begun to touch the edge of the field. On both sides of the road leading to the house were large fields peppered with KEEP OUT signs. It was those large grassy playgrounds marked KEEP OUT that invoked the children's curiosity. Like fish to water, the children headed straight for the gap, helping each other through the barbed wire. Laughing at the scattering of quail and flying grasshoppers, Amber squealed in delight, "They look like popcorn popping." Mother never noticed.

And, true to what the girls had surmised, their mother reached over and cut off the stove, so relieved to hear from her husband and to tell him of the strange personalities she had encountered earlier today in town. Everyone kept to themselves. No one even appeared to have pets. The playground and park were always empty. Living at the end of town had its advantages. No one ever came out this way. Their new lone house at the end of a dead-end street stood out like a beacon with its yellow picketed fence and freshly painted forest green shutters. They had jumped at the chance to be closer to home, and the price fit their budget. The yard would need work, and their father was planning on getting some leave to get to the growing honeydue list. The soil was of chert, made of clay and rock and with the large leaves shading the growth of sun-loving plants, the ground appeared barren and dismal. This would be one of his bigger projects.

Out of breath, the two reached the end of the field – a vast contrast from their yard. The long summer had brought forth an array of flowers and long blades of grass. Flowering shrubs and perennials traversed the field. Long sage reached their navels. Tall blades tickled their legs as they began to run toward the majestic grove of dogwood lining the back acreage. Grasshoppers exploded like popcorn, often sailing over the girls' heads. A covey of quail burst from nowhere and sent Amber falling backward. Taking turns, they began a game of hide and go seek. Completely hidden by the tall grass, the girls crawled around on the ground, with only the periodic movement of disturbed small white and yellow butterflies exposing their location.

As Amber picked off the last huckleberry from her socks, she noticed her older sister staring absently at the dogwood grove. This gave Kelly an idea. Kelly motioned Amber forward, "This won't take long." Kelly reached the entry first and pointed out what appeared to be an old forgotten path, carpeted with dark green moss. The aroma from the flowers, intoxicating, prodded the children down the path. The path was narrow and cave-like. Honeysuckle vines hung overhead swaying in the summer breeze.

Back at home, still unaware of the children's disappearance, their mother remained on the phone. A concerned look, however, darkened her face. Loudly, she could be heard recanting her ventures into town, "No one is friendly. I never see children out playing. Amber and Kelly have not made any friends. Honey, I don't think this is the right place for us. There's an eerie silence I noticed this afternoon. Please hurry home."

Always the leader, Kelly began down the path, turning her head back occasionally to see Amber was still following. The branches overhead were thick, with large green leaves, blocking out the late afternoon sun. Looming overhead, the limbs formed a cathedral-like canopy. The temperature was a bit cooler. Both girls noticed how incredibly quiet everything seemed to be. As they intruded further down the path, neither heard a sound. Not a bird, the wind, or a whisper. The moss' creeping ground cover, soft and thick, appeared to absorb the sound of their steps.

In town, shop keepers were flipping the closed signs on, bolting their doors and locking up. One could watch the last-minute sweeping of porches, shades being drawn, and collecting of mail. As the minutes ticked by, the town was winding down and becoming quiet. No cars were on the road. No one was outside. The trees stood still. No dogs were barking. No birds flying. The quiet was deafening. Where was everyone going? There was a carnival.

It was a moment or two before the girls were out of sight from the entrance on the path. Brushing back a long hanging branch, Kelly emerged first, followed by Amber into a large lush clearing. Kelly saw it initially, and shouted with excitement, "Look, it's beautiful!"

Amber pushed past Kelly and fell into the deep green carpet. "It's everywhere!" she added. Both grabbed handfuls and playfully threw handmade balls of soft green moss at each other. Tasseling in the pasture of moss, Kelly and Amber fell to their knees. The forest trees formed a large circle around the greenest, thickest moss ever seen. A low rhythmic beat could be heard coming from the center of the sphere of moss. "Do you hear that?" Amber asked.

"No," her sister responded. "What are you talking about?" Kelly picked a handful of moss up and took a big whiff. "Wow, this stuff smells sweet!" Turning, Kelly exclaimed, "Look, Amber, I'm a frog!"

"Hahaha, you look so funny," Amber said with a grin. Kelly had smeared the green moss over her face, the green moss now concealing her clear complexion. Her white teeth beamed through a haze of green. Amber quickly followed, wiping the moss across her face. "And, I'm a leprechaun!" Both fell to the ground in a fit of giggles. They were both snickering when Amber noticed she couldn't rub the green color off her hands and face. Showing concern, Kelly found she couldn't rub off the green moss stains either. Kelly moaned. "Mother is going to kill us!"

"I'm not worried about Mother," stated Kelly, "but this stuff is not coming off!" Her skin began to tickle and then burn. "Amber," she screamed, "I can't get it off!" She could see from the corner of her eye, her sister crying and swatting at her face attempting to stand.

Amber whimpered, "Kelly, help me!" She couldn't get the burning moss off. An overwhelming fear crept over them.

Neither had noticed the forest trees closing in behind them. The path was no longer visible. The sweet smell from the flowers now changed to the stench of burning skin. No one could hear their screams or the gurgling sounds from the forest. It didn't take long – everything fell silent.

The sun was setting when Mother stepped out onto the porch. "Girls, dinner!" Mother called one more time from the porch. *Where are they*, she wondered. Mother ran back in to cover the steaming rice and to cut off the eyes. The ice in the glasses had already begun to melt from the heat of the long hot summer day now coming to an end. "It's almost supper time," she said aloud. "They know we eat at six." Wringing her hands, she paced back and forth in front of the window. Glancing at the clock, she decided to go in search of them. She grabbed her sweater off the stairway post and held it tightly as if it would offer protection. She walked briskly out the door, catching her breath as she heard the door slam behind her. She circled the house and down the walk to the mailbox.

"Girls, dinner!" She had not gone far when she thought about the field. She had forbidden her children weeks ago, not to play in the field. She stopped at the fence. Nothing moved! Not even the wind. Even though sweat beaded across her brow, she felt a chill and shuddered. Collecting her skirt, she climbed over and proceeded across. The long blades of milkweed cut across her legs, depositing seeds sticking like tape. The low hum from the crickets grew and lessened as if the field was a large heart. The continuous pounding grew so loud that Mother could no longer hear the beating of her own heart.

"Amber, Kelly!" she shouted to break the sequence. "Amber, Kelly! Oh God, answer me!" Her mind raced at all the possibilities when children go missing. Time was running out. Overwhelmed with fear, she began to cry. Finally, reaching the end of the field with tears streaming down her face, she noticed a small path. In the distance, one could hear the town's clock strike one. In front of her, she could see a clearing, but no tracks. She began in that direction. Strike two. In all her despair, she began to smell the scent of the honeysuckle. Intoxicating. Beneath her feet, she felt herself step onto a lush green carpet. Strike three. Her mood lifted and she slowed down. She moved back a low hanging branch and came into a clearing that had this aura of content. Everything looks so beautiful and lush. She didn't even hear the fourth chime. Bending down to admire the thick moss, she grabbed a handful and brought it close to her face and pressed it against her tear-stained cheeks. Strike five. "Oh," she said. Rising suddenly, she dropped the handful. She wiped her hands across her chest. She looked at her watch. She turned to see the forest swallow the path. Her screams were blocked by the sixth chime. It was 6 pm. Dinner.

When he finally arrived home, he parked his cruiser and walked into an empty house. They hadn't been there long, but he was trying to fit in, working with the after-school programs. He regretted not spending more time with his family, but they were good, right? He stood at six feet. He was slim but muscular. He kept his face clean-shaven and his hair cut short. He liked things neat, ship-shaped, and orderly. He cringed at the thought of all those boxes he still had not unpacked. He knew he had got his priorities turned around and placed work before family. It was hard to do the right thing, all the time. If only he could persuade others that you just keep trying. The lights and television were on in the living room. When he strode into the kitchen, he observed the stove was off, and the food once hot, was lukewarm. The ice in the glasses had completely melted. "Hello?" he repeated. He stepped out on the back porch and scanned the horizon and saw nothing amiss. He climbed the stairs and preceded into their bedroom. He pulled off his pistol, belt, holster, and badge, placing them carefully in the side safe. With children in the house, one always needed to be careful; he was no different. He changed into his favorite orange T-shirt, the one with his graduate UT design. He pulled out his cell phone to check his messages. None were there. He made a mental note to grab his wife's boxes and bring them upstairs. At first, he wasn't worried, but when he walked into the garage and saw the Buick was still there, the hair on the back of his neck stood up. "Don't panic," he told himself.

He started to recount his day and movements. "When was the last time we talked?" he asked himself. Remembering he had told her about the missing boy earlier, "Around 4 pm, right? Yeh. 4 pm. OK – everything was OK at 4 pm." He looked at his watch, that was two hours ago. He walked out to the mailbox and saw nothing more than a late afternoon sun going down, and the heat of the day starting to fade. Standing there, the anxiety of the day settling on his shoulders, and you could see the slump. He had so much on his plate, never sure if he was doing it right, but feeling his way along. He wondered how he had gotten to where he was.

He called his mom. She was the number three on his emergency contacts. They hadn't talked in a long time, but he was trying not to panic and needed a little distraction. She answered on the second ring. She was driving back in her truck from a long day and seeing his ID, picked up the phone. Like all her kids, he didn't call when things were great, so she was hesitant and braced herself. She turned the radio off.

"Hi Honey!" It was a sudden release of uneasiness, hearing her voice; it made him smile. It only lasted a few moments. "What's wrong?" He felt stupid telling her his fears and wondering where his wife and kids were. She kept quiet, listening to every detail. She questioned if he had looked around the house, the neighborhood, and the fields. Making a list in his head, he assured her he was going to repeat some of those places and go further with her suggestions. He kept the phone to his ear, walking and calling out their names. Periodically, his mother would ask, "Where are you now?" and he would recant where he had progressed. And then the strangest of questions came, one that he wasn't expecting. "Did they have on their pendants?"

The question hit him like a load of bricks. He didn't know. His pager went off, and it startled him. "I've got to go, Mom," he said, hanging up the phone. He ran back upstairs, taking two at a time. Throwing his uniform back on, he glanced at the alarm clock, wondering again, *where are they?*

When he got to the station, he went down the lime green hall covered with wanted posters to the report room. A four-walled classroom-sized area with a tornado fan in the corner still going on high was where they all got their news and duty assignments. The three long white tables were lined up in rows with four to five chairs at each table. Others were already in the room, some talking with their buddies, others scrolling through their iPhone waiting for the chief. He took a chair in the back. It wasn't but a few moments later when their boss walked in. "OK – everybody here?" Not really looking up to see what the answer was, he focused on his clipboard in his hand.

"Guys, we have a missing child in our area. The mother had filed a missing person. Here's the latest picture." He passed it to the first officer on his right. "He was last seen walking away from his house. He's been missing since noon. He was wearing jeans and a white T-shirt, about 4 ½ feet tall. Brown hair, brown eyes. Guys, this little boy is autistic and shy. I need you guys to pull some extra hours and see if we can get this knocked out."

With that, the echoed sounds of chairs scraping the floor and the movement of people walking out were all that was heard. They were a focused bunch. No one asked any other questions, but you could see the seriousness on their faces as many were aware of this little boy and his mother's situation. This was a small enough town that everyone knew a little about everyone, whether they wanted to or not. The captain handed them their zones to check out. Those that had vehicles started on the farther end of town, while those walking or with bikes took the inner perimeters of the town. Which explains how the veteran ended up going to the older boy's home, the one he had seen earlier that morning from the drugs at school. He had an inkling to ask him about the pendants again – as things were starting to raise the hair on his neck and he wondered if that kid had been out at his place. But he didn't see him.

By the time he came back from his perimeter checks, he had nothing to report. The next shift of officers were coming in. He called home again, but no one picked up. Now really worried, he stopped by his boss' office and tapped on his door which was opened. "Hey, I may have a situation too," he said, walking in and taking a seat.

Strawberry Fields Forever

Driving past the city's sign, both kids glanced at each other and smiled. They had been passing miles of yellowish-brown fields for what felt like forever. They had passed numerous farmlands peppered with grassy pastures, cotton, and grazing cows. Mom always liked to take the back roads, avoiding crowds and traffic as much as possible. This kept them on the two-lane country roads, but it was the spectacular view of the landscape which kept their attention most of the time. They wondered if they would be able in the future to investigate the small-town charm they had heard of. Each had struggled to share the blanket and for a comfortable spot to sleep off and on during the drive. They both had been scolded earlier when they got into a thumping game, each squaring off with finger flicks, leaving small welts and future bruises on their arms and legs. It was fun – until it wasn't. The air conditioner had never worked, so all four windows were down, circulating and blowing the hot summer air through the car as it traveled. They knew they had finally arrived when they felt the car slow down and heard the turn signal clicking. They had heard stories most of their lives about their grandmother but had never had the chance to visit before. She lived so far south and in a very interesting part of the country. It was a very secluded spot; they were excited to explore and had a million questions. To be honest, they had been cautioned about her strange methods, and being kids, this just intrigued them.

Grandma insisted she be called Momma C. Her meticulous approach to every facet of her life became quite obvious to the kids when they observed the neat rows of fields, manicured lawns, and her incessant habit of grabbing hold of the children's shoulders and reminding them to sit up.

Every year around this time, Grandma's fields produced the world's reddest, juiciest, and largest strawberries. They had been told she had a secret on how and why the strawberries were so unique. But she never let on to what that secret was, and held it close.

The day was coming to an end when they reached her driveway. It was long, sweeping, and lined with electric fencing. This was to keep animals out, their mother explained. The sunbeams peeking through the tall pines cast shadows across the fields. Two large barking dogs came bounding up the drive and met the car. Apparently trained to keep intruders out, their sharp white teeth were a bit alarming when they jumped up on the car doors. Instantly, both children rolled their windows up.

Their mother had not been home in years. In fact, her mother had started the strawberry business after Maggie had left for college. She was unaware of the vast fields, barns, and the business. But she wanted to know more. She had missed her mom. It had been particularly hard when her husband had died suddenly. And it was too much when it came to raising two children and trying to keep a household together while mourning the love of her life. She had packed all they had left. She sold most off to cover the bills. She would have to get a job soon. She was worried. The children, too, quickly realized this was far more than visiting with Momma C; her business had grown over 2,000 acres, half of it appeared as elaborate rows of strawberries and the other half were dark woods.

Their grandmother was standing on a deep front porch tending to the hanging ferns when the station wagon came to a stop. An inviting white wooden swing swayed in the breeze. They could hear her call the dogs back into the house. Responding to her command, the dogs ran up the porch and into the house where the children observed the door close. The kids then came barreling out of the car. "Grandma! Grandma!" And with open arms, she hugged them tightly. She smelled of soap. Her hair was all white and pulled back into a tight bun. She wore pants that were rolled up on the ends and a plaid shirt buttoned all the way up. She wore an odd silver necklace with a pendant that resembled a small lump of coal. Digging into her pant pockets, she handed each child a gift, "Here, put these on." The gifts were duplicates of the necklace she wore. Before she had finished fastening the tender chain around their necks, both got a whiff of some smell that neither could identify; they discussed that at length prior to falling asleep later that night.

Gathering the suitcases and garbage bags of clothes, they all entered the house. It was cool, comfortable, and inviting. The children spread out to explore the rooms. One of the first things they noticed were the large circulating ceiling fans practically in every room. These caused lighter weight objects to move gently with the fabricated breeze.

The living room's tabletops were covered with old framed photos and newspaper clippings. "Don't touch those," she reminded the children, "I save them for your grandfather." A cadre of other styles lined the walls with stuffed animal trophies and an odd assortment of plates, paintings, and candles.

Maggie leaned down and whispered into their ears, "They never throw anything away."

"Where's grandpa?" Maggie queried. She immediately felt guilty. She had not returned and had only written letters and sent bouquets of fruits and flowers over the years. *What was wrong with me*, she thought to herself. *My parents deserved better*, she continued to think to herself. She turned to look at her mother who responded.

"He's up in his room, dear. That's where he's most comfortable. Go up and see him after dinner." Her father never recovered from the attack. He had been working out in his yard when two tattooed men appeared from nowhere asking for directions. They brazenly attacked him from behind with a hammer, pushing him down to the ground and knocking him unconscious. The two escaped convicts had managed to break away from the penitentiary a few days earlier and had been holding up in the woods. Both had extensive criminal histories that included gang slayings, gun-related offenses, drug possession, and theft. They spent the next few hours rummaging around the farm for his money, as they ransacked the house for items and cash and killed the dog. Thank goodness Momma C wasn't there. She was the one who discovered him, and what unfolded over roughly a two-hour period afterward has never been revealed. His graphic injuries described an unleashed evil across his ravaged body. He had fought as best he could against his armed intruders, but the multiple injuries sustained left him struggling to hold on. It had been Momma C who for the last nine years has been nursing him back to life, helping him through his suffering nightmares, pain, and frustration as he was forced to live in a bed.

"I prepared dinner, I knew you two would be hungry," she said as she walked in with a steaming platter of a hearty oven-baked chicken covered with apple-wood smoked bacon. The aroma had their mouths watering. "You must eat your vegetables before you can have dessert. And before you ask, it's my favorite, blackberry cobbler." The two stared at the vegetables she already had on the table and squirmed. Crispy Brussel sprouts and the pan-roasted okra just like their mother had warned them about. Maggie smiled from across the table. "Enjoy," she mouthed.

Dinner was good and gone. Maggie was particularly glad the children had not attempted to lick their plates, as the scraping of the forks had already caused Momma C to look up twice. The children asked to be excused, but Momma C shook her head, "No. Help me clean up first." With that, they picked up their dishes and carried them into the kitchen. It must have been the first time they had ever gone into the kitchen. It looked like a wonderland of solid white. Everything in the pantry was lined up neatly in mason jars. This was where both were sure Momma C got her inspiration for creative cooking, as it truly reflected her personality. The shiplap walls, quartz counters, gas stove, and tiled floor were all white. Neither kid could make out what were in some of the jars and gave each other a quizzical eyebrow.

The long center island resembled a large chopping block made of solid wood. They fingered the indentions left from hard and deep whacks from an obviously sharp blade. On the counter was a lone 1980s radio clock also made of wood. It was one of those older versions with dials and knobs to turn up the volume, switches to AM or FM, and a tuner for station searches. It was on, the sound was barely audible. "Want me to turn off the radio, Momma C?"

She stopped and turned around, giving a flat answer, "No."

Maggie had taken this time to venture on her own through the house and up to her father's room. The door was closed but she could see the light peering out from below and knew he was still awake. She tapped lightly on the door and thought she heard a sound, so she entered. The lamp at the bedside was on and he was lying there with his eyes closed. She watched the covers move with his breathing. There was a moment of hesitation, where she thought that perhaps she should leave, until he spoke in a very small voice, "Hi, honey."

"Hi, Daddy." She moved closer and reached for his small hand, giving it a loving squeeze. The healed but visible scars across his face and arms were etched in his weathered skin. The room was warm and smelled of lavender and ole spice. His hair was longer and she remembered he had always kept it short. That was different. She could tell her mother had taken the time to make sure he was surrounded by familiar things. She looked around and smiled, seeing his plaques and awards mounted on the walls. The heavy décor of dark warm furniture consisted of a wrought iron canopy bed, two bedside tables – one covered with numerous medicine vials and bottles, the other with books and a lamp, and a pen and paper. A long tube hanging in the upper corner of the headboard revealed an opaque bag draining its chalky white content under the covers. She suspected this is how Mom fed him. His window, although closed, had open drapes, allowing the moonlight to cast its light across the floor. She leaned in to kiss him on the forehead and noted the same necklace around her father's neck. "How are you doing, Daddy?" He responded with a thumbs-up sign but didn't really attempt to speak. "I love you. I'm so sorry I haven't seen you. I have missed you so."

He squeezed her fingers; it was a gentle touch and a flood of memories came surging back. She did most of the talking, recanting some laughable moments, forcing herself to sound more optimistic and upbeat. She left him sleeping after some time had passed. She was exhausted. Closing his bedroom door, she turned and started toward her room. It was comforting seeing her sheets of the bed turned down, and a small lamp on. Mom thought of everything. She started to undress when there was a tap at her door.

"Yes?" Walking over, she opened the door. "Oh, hi Mom. Thank you for dinner."

Momma C stood at the doorway with an outstretched hand, "Here honey, this is for you." It was a necklace, warm from being in Momma C's hand, "Put this on."

"Thank you, Mom. I will." She leaned over and gave her a hug. "Thank you for allowing us to do this."

Her mother smiled and whispered, "Justice prevails."

Maggie closed her door and went back to readying for bed. Her bedroom had a full bathroom attached. The glossy white large claw-foot soaking bathtub looked so inviting. She turned on the faucets filling the tub, placing the necklace on the counter. Slipping into the warm pool, she could feel the aches from the day easing. She knew Mom would take care of the kids tonight. She so needed this and closed her heavy and tired eyes. This would become a repeated ritual over the next few days. She felt that she was finally able to sleep and wondered, *am I catching up on lack of sleep for the past few months? Can one do that?*

"Get into bed and get some sleep, we have a big day tomorrow." Leaving the kitchen, the two headed upstairs to their room they shared. The room held two bunked beds with numerous layers of quilts, coverlets and blankets, a fireplace, one large window that opened out to the fields, and a small bathroom. The walls were painted a confederate gray, with egg shelled drapes and window trim. Their suitcases and garbage bags of clothes and possession on the wood floor reminded them how offbeat their world had been of late. Each found their belongings and changed into pajamas. They both skipped washing and brushing their teeth; neither would rat on the other. Climbing into their beds, they were fast asleep within moments of their heads hitting the pillows. The day had been long.

Momma C had stayed in the kitchen; she was listening to the radio intently. Her head tilted looking down, adjusting her belt. Moments passed, but from a distance, an observer watched her get up and call out to her dogs. They immediately appeared, and she opened the back door and let them out, where she followed them.

Morning came early. Dawn was breaking and the condensation on the grass and steamy looking fog from the rows of plants was visible but quickly evaporating. It would be another hot day. Momma C had already fed the dogs and walked them across the main field. Her dogs had massive heads and powerful hindquarters and she used them for guarding and hunting. She counted on their determined build in that particular breed of dog to keep her and those she loved safe. They seemed very interested in one particular section this morning, and Momma C was curious to know what they had picked up on. Both dogs circled one large tree on the far end of the field and sat, drawing her attention. She walked over and looked down. Three cigarette butts and tracks near the trunk. *Hmm*, she thought and smiled at the dogs. She peered back at the house and could see from that angle into the kitchen as the blinds were up. Making a note to herself, she needs to ensure she puts those down at night. They continued to walk the fence line, saw no damages, and walked back to the house.

The smell of bacon woke the kids. Still in their pajamas, they came bounding down the stairs. Sounding like a herd of elephants, Momma C made another mental note, *they need to learn not to walk on their heels*. She met them at the entryway into the dining room, smiling. "Come and get it!" They moved past her so quickly, it swirled her around. There on the table was a heaping platter of scrambled eggs, fresh-squeezed orange juice, and a mound of streaming pancakes with pads of butter sliding off the sides and pooling. The kids forked over serving after serving, leaving Momma C wondering if she had made enough.

"Yeah, Mom, they eat a lot," said Maggie, coming in from behind, looking for coffee to jump start her day. She was wearing what she had slept in which was her husband's old striped dress shirt. She had done that when they first started living together, and it just felt comfortable and so she never stopped. From the dining room window, Maggie caught a glimpse of the field hands already out in the strawberry fields. Working groups of men and women covered with gloves, large straw hats, and scarves, tilling the rows, picking and spraying the plants. They looked, from her direction, like beekeepers, covered from head to toe.

"How long do they work the fields?" Maggie asked, sipping from the mug of hot brew her mother handed her. A perfect cup doctored with cream and sugar. It tasted good.

"Oh, they come in at the crack of dawn and work till they're done," her mother answered. She picked up the empty plate of pancakes and eggs and started toward the kitchen.

"I didn't know strawberries were sprayed. Is that the secret formula to keeping them so lush?" Maggie teased.

"That's part of it, dear." Turning toward the children, Momma C started picking up the empty glasses, "You guys need to get ready, so go get dressed and meet me by the truck. I have got to go into town, and you guys are going with me." Jumping up with excitement, the two took off back to their room. Looking across the table at her daughter, she added, "Maggie, you can stay here and rest up; you looked so tired last night. So, give yourself a break. I'll take the kids with me this morning. If you're hungry, the eggs are in the refrigerator. Your children polished off the rest."

"Did I tell you 'thank you', Mom?"

"Yes, dear, you did – several times." Returning back from the kitchen, Momma C stopped back at the table, standing next to Maggie, "Will you check on your daddy while I'm out?"

"No problem, Mom."

Moments later, the kids were heard outside by the truck, chattering excitedly about what they could possibly be going to see and do with their grandmother. They wondered where her dogs were but didn't see them. Maybe she puts them up when the field workers were there? The morning was still cool with a slight breeze, but you could tell it was going to quickly become a hot day. Red and green hummingbirds flitted back and forth between the rows of small white flowers scattered across the tops of the strawberry fields.

Momma C came out the side kitchen door, her arms loaded with trays. She was wearing her usual, a buttoned-up top and a pair of jeans. She really didn't look her age, which the children weren't sure they really knew. Momma C's large black Silverado extended cab looked like a monster and they were thrilled to be able to ride in it. The kids climbed into the back seats, each taking a window. Her comfortable leather seats and air conditioner were a lot nicer than what they had been used to and they took care not to leave scuff marks from their shoes. The kids heard the back tailgate close and wondered what Momma C had loaded into the back.

Climbing up into the driver's seat, she motioned for the children to buckle up. She turned the radio on to the local music station catching the last tunes of one of their favorite songs, and off they went. The workers in the field never looked up.

Maggie finished her first cup and went for another. The mister coffee still left on brew was burning the few drops left in the pot. Already the kitchen was full of the burnt aroma, so she opened the window. As hard as Maggie tried, she couldn't spot a clean spoon to mix the sugar in the instant coffee she began to prepare as her second cup. "How does Mom do this?" She started upstairs to go check on her father and grabbed the newspaper off the table in the dining room to take to him.

Driving through the town's square, with their noses pressed up against the window, the children observed the two-story buildings lining the square of all sides. The second stories had balconies and pretty window displays. Bountiful cars and trucks parked in neat rows with individual meters ticking away left room for others. The township had invested tall lights and planters with overgrown vegetation hanging over the pots' sides. The flowers were an array of red tulips, yellow perennial, and blue iris. It was their first time to see the Confederate statue – the soldier was looking down South Lamar, and at its feet were cannonballs.

The first stop Momma C made was the town's post office. All of the occupants bailed out of the truck and up the stone steps to the front office. The massive red-bricked building had been built in 1856 and heralded an interesting history as it had not always served as a post office but a warehouse for trades. During the civil war, it had been burned to the ground, and in 1872, it had been rebuilt. Inside the federal building foyer, the walls were lined with pictures of the FBI's most wanted. Interestingly enough, Momma C stopped and surveyed the black and white pictures which made the children curious to know what that meant. Several mean looking characters with scary descriptive language written under the photos had big red Xs across their faces. "What does that mean?" they both asked in unison.

"What, the red Xs?" Momma C questioned for clarity. She reached into her front pocket. Nodding and responding a "yes" and a "yeah," the children prodded her to answer.

"Well, those are the ones they are no longer looking for. All of these are bad men. They have harmed people, friends, and family." Looking past the children and around the room, ensuring no office employee was looking, she quickly took the red marker out and crossed over a face on the wall.

"Momma C, you can't do that!" they said, shocked that their grandmother was defacing public property. She threw them a quick sheepish grin and moved them along outside. The sun was out and bright which left them all squinting and shielding their eyes as they continued walking to the truck, so they didn't see anyone in particular. They were unaware of the high school-aged boy that passed directly in front of them heading into the post office. The sidewalks were already starting to heat up and the grass looked crispy and brown in spots where dog walkers had been. So they moved quickly toward the truck and were relieved by the air conditioner.

"Our little secret, OK?" Somehow, at that very moment, knowing that their grandmother had done something sneaky, they bonded. Momma C had a secret, and now she was sharing it with them. They both shared smirks and snickered – this was too great. They could never let their mother know and would never tell.

Loading back into the truck, they headed toward the far end of town. They were enjoying the view of the town's square, shops, and tree-lined sidewalks. It was a pretty town, they could tell that. The town had a square, with great sidewalks to walk around its borders. Some of the shops were the types of cafés where you can eat outside on the wrought iron tables and chairs and under large shading umbrellas. The store windows were large and there were pretty and decorative displays of clothes, paintings, and other wares. The traffic was light and moving slowly to allow the walkers access across streets. The town itself felt friendly. She continued out past the city's welcome sign, down a long highway toward the far end of the county. "What's out there?" the youngest queried. From the backseat, they could see and hear the lights and sounds of a carnival.

"This is where the town is right now – we love to enjoy the carnival," she said. Momma C turned and smiled, "I've got to drop off a shipment of strawberries to the vendors at the carnival. Do you guys want to stay for a bit and ride some rides?" This was turning out to be the best day in a very long time and they were excited to be a part of it. She parked the truck next to the other vehicles already parked. As they exited the truck, they helped Momma C unload the trays packed with strawberries and walked them over to the food vendors who were busy preparing the grills and picnic tables. Momma C introduced the children to her clients and they all acknowledged the usual greetings and continued to busy themselves with preps. The crowds were starting to move through the front gates looking forward to rides and treats. Momma C reached down in her pocket and pulled out several dollar bills and instructed the children to go to the ticket booth and choose their rides. This was so much fun!

As they were all standing in line, the children noticed a small little boy standing next to his mother. Well, actually they heard him first, which made them turn. He was humming. He looked scared. Momma C gave him a smile; it appeared she recognized him and walked back toward the boy. At first, she offered him a strawberry. But he hid behind his mother's frame and avoided eye contact.

"I'm sorry, I didn't mean to scare him," Momma C stated to the mother. His mother, small in frame, was wearing a floral dress, with the hem of her slip showing from the little boy holding and pulling at her waist. She reached down and gathered his hands.

"Oh, it's OK. He's a little shy, but thank you for the strawberry. I'll take it and give it to him later," his mother responded politely.

"Well actually, I'd like to give him this. Tell him it's special." From her pocket, she pulled out another gift; it was a necklace – and placed it in the mother's hand.

Momma C and the children then moved forward to the front of the line and purchased their tickets. "Momma C, do you know that boy?" queried her grandchildren.

Looking straight ahead, she answered, "No, not exactly, but he lost his father several years ago and his mother had been raising him all by herself. It's always good to be nice to those who are struggling."

He had followed them to the carnival. He was out of breath when he got to the front gates as he had ridden his bike, and it was hot and dusty down those long back roads. He saw that old woman with a couple of kids heading toward the ticket counter and then over to the younger-looking woman with the funny-looking kid. The older woman handed something to the kid which he didn't take and hid behind his mother's skirt.

There were so many rides, sights, and sounds that it was hard for the kids to decide what they would do first. Scanning the horizon, they spotted the Ferris wheel and pulling and pointing, they dragged Momma C toward the first of many rides. The popcorn smells wafting through the air hit their senses, and two bags later were completely consumed, chased down with cokes. They continued to wander into the crowd, deeper toward more attractions and games. Momma C took out her phone to call Maggie and update her on what and where they were. She then proceeded to take pictures of the children and their new painted faces. Midday, they discovered the makeshift water ride which sprayed a sprinkler overhead, hitting their hot faces and smudging their fresh artwork. They rode that one twice until their shoes were soaked. All one could really see were just big grins and a sense of lost time. Breathless and skidding into the next line and booth, they all continued on. They pinged back and forth from ride to ride the whole afternoon. They were having a much-needed break from the past and this was turning out to be a perfect day.

On the way home, the children fell asleep, still wearing the smeared painted faces and particles of food from the endless array of funnel cakes, fries with ketchup, and steaming hotdogs. They had not been camera shy when it came to snapping some memories up. She tried to catch their smiles on the rides and felt pleased that Maggie would like them. She would add these to the mantel and in Granddaddy's room. He would like that too. They left the crowds of revelers and headed home. They were unaware of what happened an hour later to one of the carnival vendors later that night but heard it on the news the next day.

Maggie surprised her mom and the children. The day for her had been great and restful. Energized, she decided to make dinner, probably not as elaborate as Mom's, but making the attempt to feel normal again. And who didn't like macaroni and cheese with sweet tea? The table with some of Mom's favorite napkins and platter ware was easy enough to set and she felt proud that she pulled off the color scheme. The steamy cheesy aroma drifted out the front door. She pulled the hot bowl out of the oven and stuck a large spatula in the middle. Pulling into the driveway, they fell out of the truck, still laughing and smiling from the day, and met their mother at the front door. "We smell macaroni!"

This is what a family should come home to, she thought, amazed that after eating tons of junk food and drinks at the carnival, these two would still be hungry, but they were.

It's All a Balancing Act

The house was quiet. After dinner, the kids nearly fell asleep at the table, nodding but still shoving food into their mouths. "OK, guys, it's time for bed." Neither had said another word but rolled out of their chairs and up to bed. Maggie too had been tired and quickly loaded the dishes in the dishwasher and headed up to her room for a nice lavender soak. Steaming hot water reddened her skin and made her sweat a bit. She could feel her muscles relaxing and closed her eyes.

Maggie awoke. She had fallen asleep in the tub. The water was now cold. But it wasn't the water that woke her. "Did I hear something?" she queried. She wrapped her towel around her shivering body and dripping, climbed out of the tub. She went to her window and peered out. The clouds had moved in, blocking the moon's light. She wasn't sure, but she thought she saw something moving along the far end of the field lined with trees. It was so dark, it could be an animal. "Yes, there it is again… What in the world?"

Maggie thought she could make out her mother's form walking with the dogs. She was watching her walk along the tree line, when her attention was drawn to another, behind her mother. A few yards back. It looked like it was moving fast up to her, from behind. Suddenly, the flashlight that had been lighting her mother's way went out. Maggie now could see nothing.

The scene sent a jolt through her body. By the time she had thrown on her jeans and a shirt and darted out the back door, her mother was nowhere to been found. She had no light and started to call out to her mom, searching in the dark. She was pretty sure no one could hear her from the house and thought about her iPhone sitting there on the bedside table, charging. *Darn it*, she thought and contemplated running back into the house for a flashlight and her phone. She continued to look around and shout out her mother's name. Neither her mom nor the dogs responded. The moon cast very little light as the weather appeared to be getting darker and colder.

She had been walking along the edge of the field squinting her eyes to attempt to make out objects when she detected a narrow light coming from one of the distant barns. The door, slightly ajar, let out a small beam of light – barely seen from the distance. Maggie started making her way in that direction, still hearing nothing but the wind and nocturnal animals hooting, chirping, and screeching. As creepy as the night was turning out, the field seemed to be alive.

As she reached the door of the barn, she called out again to her mother. It was then as her mother who was crouched down stood up and turned around, that Maggie gasped. In the center of the barn was a large metal chain hanging from the top rafters of the ceiling frames. Dangling on the end of the chain was a man, slightly swinging, upside down, his hands and feet bound, his mouth taped. He was making grunting noises of distress. Two thin tubes were inserted on either side of his neck. The ends of the tubes were fastened to two large containers, half-filled. Maggie felt sick.

"What are you doing, Mom?" she screamed. Momma C, adjusting the tubes, ignored the anguished cry of pain filling the air and his withering in agony.

"Maggie," she started and then walked closer to stand directly in front of her, blocking her view of the scene, "you don't understand." Her mother took her by the arm and guided her to sit down on the hay bales stacked along the wall.

"What's going on, Mom? Who is he? And what are you doing?"

As her mother readied herself to explain all, Maggie surveyed the room. Large bales of hay stacked to the ceiling on all sides and several large sealed canisters arranged in neat rows lined in front of the back wall were all that occupied the barn. She quickly recanted the field workers and the canisters they used for spraying; she felt sick. There was no tractor or other types of farm equipment. The two dogs sat quietly on either side of the man hanging from the chains, licking their paws. From his exposed arms and partially uncovered face, he was white, almost gray in color. His tattooed arms and scars were barely visible. They looked like gang signs, and under his left eye was an empty teardrop.

"Maggie," she started. "Maggie!" she repeated, drawing her attention. Maggie refocused and looked up at her mother. "This man is an escaped convict. Much like the ones who hurt your daddy."

"How do you know this? He could be anyone!" she quipped back, wondering seriously if her mother had gone mad.

"Maggie, this man is bad. I know this man is bad. Honey, I didn't plan on ever telling you about this."

"What do you mean, you were never going to tell me about this? What are you talking about?"

Maggie's pleading look and tear-stained face were all Momma C could see, but she stood resiliently and continued. "From the beginning? Is that where you'd like me to start?" she said, not sure Maggie could understand it all, but willing to tell her and help her through.

"Well, yeah Mom, all of it."

"OK, dear. This, all of this, started nine years ago."

"Are you kidding me?" Maggie interrupted.

"Yes, Maggie, nine years ago. Nine years ago when I found your father half dead from being terrorized and beaten. The body odor and rabid breath from his assailants still on his clothes and wounds. I pledged to your father who was fighting for his life, that I would make amends. And, I did." She hesitated for a second and added, "I made amends for you too."

"What does that mean, Mom?"

"Maggie, the truth? I made a pact with the spirits." She glanced at her watch and then back at Maggie. The night was progressing, and there was much more to complete. The spiritual laws of balance were essential and to maintain the stability of the souls in plants, rocks, wind, fire, and all life forms, the respect and the paths taken had to be secured. A life for a life.

"Oh God, Mom, what have you done?"

"I protected my family, Maggie. Just like you would have done. I have always protected my family. Who do you think took care of the men who killed your husband?"

"What?"

"Yes. You heard me. I took care of those men, who killed your husband. I had their hearts in my hand and I made them into pendants to keep evil away." Looking down at Maggie's neck, she added, "Where's your necklace?"

"I don't know, Mom," she stated exasperatedly then added, "On the bathroom counter... I don't know, I don't remember. Wait, Mom... what did you give to my children?"

"Hearts," she said flatly. Momma C was growing angry and frustrated with Maggie. "Maggie, go get that pendant on now." She pulled her daughter up on her feet and pushed her forward and out the door. "Now!" she shouted.

Momma C, pushing from behind, guided Maggie back to the house. She was worried that Maggie would not get the necklace on fast enough. Out of breath, they climbed the steps and ran to Maggie's room.

The Apple Doesn't Fall Far

He thought about his dad a lot. He never talked about it with his mom. He wondered what his dad was doing and where he was. It had been months since he had seen him last. Those visits were never long enough and he had missed a few. He knew his dad was a mean man. But somehow, he looked up to him. Before things had gotten really bad, his father would talk with him. It probably wasn't a normal conversation that other fathers have with their kids, but that's all he had and he hung onto it. The stories his dad would tell were crazy scary. He thought he made them up, but as he got older, he realized this was what his father really did. The details in which his father would recant were so vivid and he would tell it with such fervor that it was exciting and he wanted to hear more.

It was so surreal to find his dad's picture up on the wall. He had stumbled upon it while mailing out the bills and checking meters for change. His dad's picture hung up next to several other most wanted in the local post office. He grimaced every time he passed by but was still drawn to it in secret for its notoriety. It was the only picture he knew of his dad. He knew because he had turned their house upside down looking for a picture, but never found one. He was disappointed that his family was so different. His dad was sort of this burly type, with a big chest, shoulders, and neck. He wore his hair long, sometimes in a ponytail, most of it gray and thinning. With some of his visits, he noted the growing length of tattoos down his dad's arms and neck. He had a couple of outlined empty teardrops near his left eye. His dad bragged about his tats and shared how the other men had improvised needles and sliced with razors into the skin to etch out images that they felt were empowering. His arms were sort of thick but short, pulling in toward his upper frame. Coach always told the players to ensure to use the weights at different angles not to get that appearance. So he knew his dad was always lifting, but not doing it right. He didn't take correction or criticism well, so he just kept his mouth shut. He could tell the coach had been telling it right, as his body shape was different than his father's, with more tone and defined physique. Other than the facial acne he struggled with, he had the body of an athlete.

He wanted his dad to be proud of him. He took on a rougher stance at school, trying to mimic some of the toughness his father alluded too. It got him in a lot of trouble and he had been labeled a bully. He just couldn't find his way until that volunteer coach took an interest. He hated him at first and they didn't start off well. Big guy, coming in to save the day kind of persona, but then, he did come through for him and a couple of other guys that needed a push. That's how he actually got on the team, and he was competent.

He'd watch the volunteer coach show up every day, unload some of the gear, and get out there – never minding the rain, cold, or heat. A volunteer. Man, like he didn't even have to do it, but he just did. He noted the volunteer drove this mediocre car, nothing special, and always kept it locked. Once when he ran over with some of the other guys to help unload, he noticed a pistol belt and an upside-down badge in the passenger's seat. He figured the guy was either a security guard or a cop; either way, this guy never talked about himself, and was more interested in what the other boys on the team wanted to talk about. You could tell he was a good listener.

He worked hard that summer and when the coach put out the list, he saw he was the number three guy on defensive backs. He had a jersey and gear and it felt good. He never told the coach nor the volunteer about his home life or where his father was. They didn't ask either, so it was easier to mingle within the team of players. Their team had pulled together, sweated in the heat with practice, ran some great plays, and saw the results. They played other county schools and the recognition of being on the winning team was starting to get him noticed, especially by some of the girls who never gave him a second look before.

On one of his visits, he told his dad about being on the team and the girls that were starting to take an interest. His dad gave him a wink and nodded his head, then asked him if he brought his cigarettes. That was it. He didn't ask him anything further, nothing about what position he played or what the scores had been. Just more interested in the damn cigarettes and breaking free. His father would do most of the talking. He revealed to his son that he watched the guards and their routines; he counted the paces to the fences and back and measured the height of the barbed wire fences. He was working on a plan and he shared it with his son. He was going to need him to be ready. "Did you put in the box what I told ya?"

"Yeah," he said, looking from side to side, ensuring no one was too close to hear. The boy handed over the carton.

"You be there at midnight like I told ya, you hear?" he said, looking him dead in the eyes. "Tonight."

That was the last conversation they had.

That's about the time he started smoking weed again. The first joint, he found in his dad's old leather jacket, hanging up in the closet. He had gone to retrieve the jacket as the spring temperatures at night were cool and found it stuffed in the upper pocket. He had made his way across town. He had smoked it waiting for his dad. He was sure he was where he had been told to be. He waited and waited. His dad never showed up. Finally, after several hours, he left for home, snuck back in his house just before dawn, and crawled into bed, exhausted. It wasn't too long after that when he heard about the escape on the local news, but he knew things had not gone like he had been instructed and wondered if his dad was on the down low and where he was.

It was harder to concentrate on school and practice. His mother didn't seem to notice. She hated her job, herself, and the people she worked with. She was not a happy person, ever. His dad had told him once that she had been really pretty which is why they got together. Early in their relationship, she had gotten pregnant and quit school. His dad had finished high school but had hung out after graduation around the school because his dad told him the young girls like the tough guys. He bragged to his son about the leather jacket he wore and how one of the girls had told him he looked like Elvis. His mom had been in the group of girls who flirted dangerously with his dad, and somehow they linked up.

They had lived in a small trailer the first two years after his birth. His mother reminded him how her pregnancy was an onslaught of nausea and stretch marks followed by a painful birth that left her peeing on herself every time she sneezed. His father could not keep a job and after losing one job after another, they had to move in with her grandmother. His excuse each time was that his bosses were unreasonable and demanding. The relationship fizzled out. Their screaming matches and knockdown fights left nothing to salvage. He packed up one day and did not return. Neither had squabbled over custody and the boy was left to himself a lot. He never had any money on him which is why he picked up after his father's habits of stealing whatever he could find and taking it to the pawnshop for cash. He was a regular and it started at an early age. He was jealous of the kids he went to school with. They had fresh clean clothes, hot meals, and parents who wanted to hear about their day. He always had to bring in the sheet each semester with his mother's signature to receive the token hot lunch for free. There were a couple of years where she couldn't keep him in pants as he grew tall, so most of the time he wore the ankle beater he had heard kids joking about. He hated her for that. He could tell they knew some details about his life, but no one ever came right out and said anything. He thinks they were afraid. And, to be honest, he was afraid to admit how crappy his life was, but he was willing to hurt anyone who made him feel any worse than he already did.

He learned from his dad to watch his next victim. Learn their habits and routines. Then seize upon the moment. He had been watching recently this local businesswoman. She had a huge place with lots of workers and no spouse as far as he could tell. She was an older woman and lived away from town. She has to pay those workers, so he was pretty sure she would have large sums of cash at her place. He rode out to her place on a bike he had stolen, left it out in a ditch, and walked the tree line near her place. It was dark and the night was cool. He chose that night because they were not expecting rain, which meant no tracks would be left. He had watched the clouds coming in, blocking the light from the moon at times. He watched the house and for movement for a couple of hours, smoking the last of his cigarette pack and trying to stand still without disturbing too much of the reed grasses next to the fence and trees. Listening to the wild animals making calls and grunts was a bit unnerving, as he wasn't a country boy – so he wasn't sure what was making those sounds. His feet were wet with dew and it made him shiver. He could see from her open kitchen window a flurry of activity with what appeared to be cooking and cleaning. He was a bit surprised when she opened the back door and two very large dogs came out. He had not expected the dogs and quickly stepped back into the dark behind a large tree and high tailed it back to the bike. It had been a relatively easy hike through the backwoods. The heavy thickness of trees and covered hills on each side of the streams made it a good choice to lose his scent while walking in the knee-deep water. His eyes kept sweeping the surroundings ensuring nothing saw him. He worried about snakes, but at night it was cooler, so they weren't out. When he got home, he discovered he was covered in ticks and a leech. Somehow standing there in the dark bordering the woods, the deer ticks had crawled onto his clothes. He was covered. He tore off his Bon Jovi T-shirt and started picking what he could see off. After a full body check, he found additional unwelcomed and implanted ticks in his hair, groin, and legs. The leech on the back of his calf was engorged, black, and oddly shaped. He rummaged through the kitchen and bathroom drawers looking for his mother's fine-tipped tweezers and a half-used tube of a triple antibiotic ointment.

When he arrived at school the next morning, he still felt itchy from the bites but felt sure he had found all those little suckers. He smoked the remaining small joint of weed prior to going through the front metal doors and was met with a crowd of kids lined up against the red brick hallways. "What's going on?" he asked aloud to anyone who would answer.

Some kid responded, "They brought in the dogs to do a locker check."

"A locker check?" he repeated. Then he felt his energy completely sink, "Oh no."

The overhead speaker blurted out for all students to go to their first-period class. He skipped going to his locker in the next hallway and went straight to his class. The tardy bell reverberated down the long empty hall and the doors of classes closed. Nothing at first happened. Then just before the end of the first period, the principal along with the coach came to his classroom. He didn't see the principal often. He was tall and skinny and reminded him of that hee-haw character he had seen on TV – what was his name again? Oh yeh, string bean. He avoided string bean, so they never had any interaction. The teacher was motioned over to the door, where they all seemed to have a little pow-wow. Of course, all the kids in the class were watching, so everyone's attention was on him when his teacher called his name. She instructed him to leave with the principal. Avoiding eye contact with his peers, he got up, snatching his jacket and notebook. The principal met him outside the classroom. He felt the string bean's hand on his shoulder. When he turned and looked up, he thought, *this cannot be good.*

"Son, is there something you need to tell us?" the string bean asked, looking directly at him – he could make out the coffee stench from his breath. The coach who was standing next to string bean was wearing his normal uniform and cap, chewing on his redman wad pinched between his teeth and gum. The coach had his gym bag, his massive thick arms held it up and open. There, sitting on top of his change of team clothes, was a small bag of weed, small papers, and three odd pendants. The boy just looked straight ahead and said nothing. His dad had taught him to stay quiet. "They can't pin something on ya, if you ain't talking," he remembered his father saying.

The school had him sit in the counselor's office, a small room with a school's love me wall of plaques and aerial photos of the town. He sat facing the counselor's desk staring out the window, the yellow stress squeezy ball still on the corner of the desk. He thought about hurling it out the window. The door was ajar, so he could hear the secretary calling his mother and then transferring the call to the principal's phone. A few minutes passed and the principal came out, along with the coach and the volunteer that he had recognized before, except this time the volunteer was in his uniform. He was a cop! He had suspected it but wasn't sure. There he was, dark blue long-sleeved shirt and pants, black shoes, and topping it off those thin blue line sunglasses. It conveyed authority and he got it.

The police officer started to take the cuffs off his belt, but then just reached out and placed his hand on his shoulder. "You've got to come with me to the station. We've got some questions." In his other hand, now in a plastic bag, were the pendants. He could see it and thought to himself, *why did I take those ugly old things*? He couldn't really think of a reason other than he was so used to picking stuff up and stealing anything he could get his hands on. He vaguely remembered he thought he would have given it to one of the girls he was hoping would start to like him.

His mother met him at the station. He had been driven over in the squad car with the cop. She looked tired and was in her uniform. She had left her cleaning job and walked over to the station. She didn't say anything to him, just followed him into the station where they were ushered in a small room with a table and four chairs. Another cop stopped at the door and asked if they needed anything and this made him smirk. *Yeh, out of here*, he thought to himself.

After a few minutes, the volunteer cop came into the room. He sat down across from him. His mother had her hands folded across her chest, her face tight, and her nervous foot wiggling under the table. He hoped she would just keep her mouth shut. The cop started, "We found a bag of pot in your locker. Do you know how it got there?" He could feel his mother's eyes on his face. She was trying to read his expressions. So was the cop.

"Nope," he answered.

"So, you don't know how it got in your locker?"

"Nope," he repeated.

"Where did these pendants come from?" the officer queried further. He held the baggy up and there at the bottom of the bag were the pendants, one with the chain broken. He remembered. He just wasn't telling.

"I don't know," he kept his eyes focused down on the wooden table. He could see the reflection of the officer's face on the glass over the table. He didn't know if the officer could see his reflection, so he just kept watching the reflection. He tried not to blink, or look at anything else.

"You know, this can be easy, or this can be tough. Your mom may need a moment with you to explain how serious we are." And with that, the officer stood and walked out, closing the door behind him.

"Don't!" He turned to his mom. "Don't!" he repeated. "I don't even know why you came. You've never cared before. You can't help me."

Amazingly, she just sat there saying nothing. "I know what you are thinking, Mom."

Losing her ability to remain silent, she turned and screeched, "Do you? Do you? You're just like you're no good father!"

He didn't plan it. It came so swiftly, viciously knocking her out of the chair; he stood looking down at what he did. She fell so fast as she never saw it coming. A tremendous explosion across the side of her head left her seeing stars. He had seen his father backhand her but had never done that before. He stood there with his mouth gaped, staring at her. She moved slowly up from the floor and pulled herself back into her chair. The intense pain registered as she could taste the blood in her mouth. It tasted like salt and iron.

The officer came back in, completely unaware of what had occurred as the mother had her back to him. "We're going to let you go, but you have a court date on Monday. You'll need to call in the morning every day for the rest of this week as you have been temporarily expelled due to drugs in school. This follows with why you are off the team now. Here's a card with the number to call. Ask for Officer Bramlett."

He stood and snatched his jacket off the chair with his mother following him out. The boy never looked back. It was noon now. The sun was directly overhead. The sky was a brilliant blue, birds were flitting in the puddles of potholes and the flowers in the front steps were blooming. It would have been to anyone else, a beautiful day. Instead for him, the events from the week were piling up. They both walked out past the entrance, ignoring passing strangers and shops to the end of the sidewalk's corner, but then they parted. She went her way and he went his. Neither considered looking back nor saying a word.

He was halfway home when he spotted the little boy hanging onto his mother's skirt. From a distance, they looked like a happy family spending a morning out shopping and admiring the day. He was instantly resentful and bitter. He had put his head down, stuffing his hands deep in his pockets and then skipped to the side. Time had lapsed when he looked up from sulking and realized he had walked to the far edge of town. There at the dead-end street, a house with the carport garage door up and loads of unopened boxes. Jackpot.

Can I Get an Amen?

The days turned into weeks. Still on administrative leave and a suspect, the ache of loss never got better. Labeled non-commissioned, his badge and gun were taken. There was no evidence. No bodies. No motive. No witnesses. They had been out to the house several times, dust still lined many of the objects throughout, but no real leads or fingerprints. It just remained an open case. This just made him recant the previous time in Chicago. He had been so close to finding the murders, so close on their trail. And then nothing. It was as if they had dropped off the Earth. He didn't feel he had crossed any lines in the investigation but had been personal. He wanted so much to help his sister heal and to bring justice. He felt he had let her down. He stared absently up at the front yard trees, watching the yellow leaves twisting in the cold breeze, acting disoriented as they waved back and forth holding on before breaking off to join the brothers of other brown and crispy leaves on the ground. The season had changed and so had he. He had spent several hours with the local pastor – praying and hoping against hope something would transpire or with God's hand, his family would return. He shared his thoughts with the clergy – he had seen many acts of evil but all he could think about was how he didn't protect his family and now they were gone – stolen, raped, murdered; something awful he was sure. Not looking back, he packed up his bags and walked out of the house and never blinked.

He drove through town, past the square and down the long back highways, never noticing the fall colors – just the endless white and yellow lines of the roads. Paved, hill over hills, winding lone road, it mirrored his mind. He played over and over again, the conversations, the day, the searching, and the ultimate choice. No one would know what that had been. All that time alone, missing his family, feeling like he had not done right. If not by chance, a call from his mom. She had been calling every few days but staying away, giving him his space; she understood him best. She always knew when things were at their worst, and recognized when to be there or reach out. "Come home." He didn't really think about it in detail but felt it more of a summons. He had no energy, no direction, so why not? He re-holstered the gun.

When he arrived, he had no idea his sister was there with her kids. How long had it been since they had last talked? After her husband's funeral, things for him and his family got busy and just well, confusing. Another thing to feel bad about. She seemed happy to see him; he didn't remember the last time he had seen her smile. So that felt good, seeing her content. *Mom must be doing her good.* She looked different. Maggie, he remembered, used to have this wide tangle of hair, always unkempt and in a ponytail, but what he was seeing now, was a woman that appeared ageless with lush hair falling about her shoulders. Chic thinness with steel gray eyes. It wasn't her clothes (although she was completely dressed in black – T-shirt, jeans, and boots), hair, or makeup; it was her eyes that sparkled, her skin glowed, and an infectious laugh that radiated warmth. They had always had that warmth between them despite their banter growing up.

Maggie ran down the front steps and collided into her brother, wrapping her arms around his neck, so thrilled to see him, especially sharing what they both had been through. She had so much to tell him, but this wasn't the time.

Maggie half dragged her brother up the steps, calling out to her mom and the children, who from inside heard her shouts and laugher. "What is the world?" Momma C started as she met her son at the doorway. The sun's light at his back, peeking over his shoulders, hit his mother's strong attractive face. She was an unconventional beauty and he admired how she kept it all together. It was that tight hug from his mom; he felt for the first time in weeks less frazzled. She inexplicably made everyone feel better. He trusted her and knew he could count on her.

"Did you see all those fields of strawberries?" the kids quizzed. He hadn't. He really had not seen anything in the last few weeks and felt like he was just out of sorts. He made a mental note on how big they both had grown and just how healthy they looked. He immediately thought of his girls, but he pushed it back to focus on the here and now, and tried to keep up with the conversations that were coming at him from all directions.

When the chattering died down, the grownups found themselves in the kitchen. The children had left to play outside. They had made friends with Momma C's dogs;

now, throwing the tennis balls and retrieval was the new favorite activity. This had become a routine, and they spent hours outside, coming in around dinner time exhausted but hungry.

While in the kitchen, Momma C started another pot of coffee, and they all found a place around the kitchen counter. "OK – you start," Momma C said, giving him a wide plate to lay it all out there.

It took a moment, and then he took a deep breath. "Mom, they're gone. I don't know where. Just gone."

"Did you talk to them about this place? Did they know?"

"I don't remember; maybe. There was so much going on. I just don't remember if I did." His eyes watered a bit, but he fought off the urge to let it go further. Maggie could feel and see the pain on his face and reached over to hold his hand – but he moved it quickly and shoved them deep in his pockets. He felt like shutting down again.

His mother closed her eyes, and it appeared she whispered a silent prayer, then added, "What's done is done, Amen."

"Come on, let's get you unpacked," Maggie said, picking up a bag and heading out the kitchen. "Let's go see Dad."

Momma C remained in the kitchen, she had a lot on her mind. She knew her son was hurting, but there was nothing that could be done now. *There has to be balance.* "There's no other way," she said aloud.

The wind was picking up outside and the dark clouds were rolling in. The back door of the kitchen came flying open, both children and dogs came running through with their growing bare feet slapping the hard tile floors. Needless to say, so did the mud. Smiling, Momma C motioned the children out to the porch and padded with her hand, indicating to sit down on the large swing. They sat down on either side of her and she began to tell them a story. She kept her voice low. They rocked slowly, back and forth, for quite some time, each listening intently and taking in every measure of her words. She had their undivided attention. After a while, they sat there serenely, taking it all in and listening to the whip-poor-wills and the ebb and flow of the cicadas' hum. She sent one of the children up to her room to retrieve her red jewelry box and waited for his return.

Maggie had taken her brother to their father's room. She left him there to spend some one on one time with their father. It was an emotional reunion and he spent several hours in his room, so thankful he could. Over the course of the week, their uncle seemed to change, slowly emerging from his depression and loss. He took small steps, walking alone in the fields, visiting his dad and sitting down to dinners together – at first, he would just be still and listening, but later became more engaging and argumentative as the days passed. Out of his shell he emerged. He went out of his way to ensure the kids were having fun. He tied a tire swing on a massive oak near the barn, where they took turns swinging and spinning, which would make any other humans sick. He helped them set up their tent outside, where they camped under the stars. On one of their exploring excursions, foraging for herbs, they discovered a swimming hole and learned about leeches afterward. They spotted the hummingbirds flitting from flower to honeysuckle bushes. He spent most of his time in his father's library, a retreat built in the back of the house, away from the noise and the hustle of the household. From floor to ceiling, his dad had a collection of authors, art, and maps. It was good for him to have come to the peaceful sanctuary with the picturesque rural setting at every turn. There wasn't a spot on the farm that one couldn't find appealing or peaceful.

At the end of the first week, Maggie came to his room. Everyone else was out and about doing their chores or playing. It gave her some downtime and she really needed to talk with her brother. She tapped on his door. He was reading at the small desk in the corner under some ancient lamp his mother had collected. He heard her knock and chose to ignore her; he was engrossed in a book he had found. Again, she knocked, a bit longer and louder. She started to open his door, not waiting for him to answer.

"Ah, yes," he turned and said, annoyed that she just took it upon herself to come right on in.

"I need to talk with you," she said, almost pleading. He stopped drumming his fingers on the desk. She sounded serious, and he had no idea where this was going. "You're not going to believe me. I've run through this a million times in my head, and I still don't know what to do."

"Hey, hey, slow down, Maggie. What is it? Take a deep breath. Just start with one thought, OK?"

She continued half sobbing, and several nose wipes later, she sat back, exhausted, ending a very lengthy scary and worrisome tale. "So, what do you think?"

"And, all this is first hand? What happened to the man in the barn?" he prodded.

"I don't know. When I came to, days had passed. I went through the inability to speak, weakness in all my joints. My bones ached. I couldn't even stand without support and I was plagued with headaches and partial blindness."

"But Maggie, this man might be dead. Did you ever go back?"

"Well, I'm not an idiot; yeah, I went back. But nothing was there."

"Maybe it was all in your mind. I mean, it sounds as if you were really sick. Maybe the flu or something?" She looked at him, shaking her head.

"Maggie, you're describing this illness that came on so quickly; you could have been imagining all this, especially if you had a fever. Did you have a fever?" he questioned further. He was listening closely.

"I don't remember, I think I did," she responded, still puzzled. "I don't have this all figured out yet."

"OK, Maggie – let me go over this. You think Mom killed this guy, for his… his… blood." Maggie nodded.

"And," he continued, "she did this for the strawberries?" Again she nodded, with less energy; she knew it sounded crazy and said so aloud.

"It does sound crazy," he admitted. Sitting there digesting her story, he asked, "Did anyone else get sick?"

"No," she replied. "Mom took the kids under her wing and I just lay there in bed until I got better. She literally nursed me back to health. I've really got to add, I feel really good," she said, looking down at her arms and playing with the end of a strand of hair.

He was watching her and caught her looking at her reflection in the full-length mirror behind him.

"What do you want me to do?" he asked, which immediately drew her attention back to their conversation.

"Will you check it out?"

"Sure, I'll check it out." He waited for more, but she didn't add anything further. "Feel better?" he asked.

"Yes, thank you." And then she got up and left him in his room to worry over what they had just had as a conversation. He knew there was something. He knew his mother. He knew about symmetry and balance, he just couldn't figure out where the man fit into all this or his sister.

She Doesn't Know

He waited until he heard his mother's truck drive up before he left his room. He decided to leave the house and talk with her out in the open. He passed down the long large hallways of his family's art and furniture and noted everything had a story. He knew all of them. He stopped out on the porch. He could see her unloading trays from the back tailgate and he strode over to help. The kids were already close by and appeared to be fitting in, as he noted they were helping without being asked. Momma C could tell that he had something to say and motioned him over to the far end of the pavement.

"She knows something's up," he said, directly looking at his mother.

"She thinks she does, that's it," she answered. "Here, take this into the house," handing him a tray. In tandem, they walked into the kitchen. Maggie had come down and was sitting crossed legged on one of the wooden stools. She was sipping on a cup of coffee in one of those mugs with 'BE KIND' scribbled down its side. It made him smirk. No one said anything to each other, it was sort of an odd mingling. Her mother seemed distracted and went into the cupboard and pulled out one of the clear containers less than half-filled with something white. She opened kitchen drawers until she found her measuring cups and proceeded to scoop out several servings into a bowl and mix it with warm water. It resembled gruel and there was an unusual odor which she covered with a top.

"Here, Maggie. Take this up to your dad and put it in the bag. Don't forget to unlatch the clamp."

Maggie was pouring her second cup of coffee, but stopped and put the cup down. "Ok, Mom," she responded, giving her brother a knowing look. She took the bowl, being careful not to spill any of the contents up to his room. Maggie found her dad asleep and tiptoed to the other side of his bed. She had taken the bag down and leaned it against the lamp to keep the opening up. She was just about to pour the mixture in when she jumped with a start; her father had reached over and touched her leg. "Daddy! Geez, that scared me."

His body was still, but his eyes were moving, looking at the door and then her. It was almost telepathic, but she felt he wanted her to close his door. Which is why she walked over and did just that. When she returned to his side, he peered at her. "You look different," he said softly.

"Do I?" she asked, curious that he too noticed a change.

"Yes," he said flatly. She unlatched the lock and saw the white mixture flowing down through the tube.

"What is this stuff you are fed, Dad?" she said, looking more intently at the grainy appearance of the mixture.

"I don't know, but it keeps me alive like your mother does." Shaking her head in agreement, she thought *Mom does a good job there.*

"You know I got sick and Mom took care of me recently," she said, looking for him to provide an answer.

"Hmm," he said, closing his eyes.

"Dad, is there something going on that I don't know about?" she said, keeping her eyes focused on his face.

He kept his eyes closed. "No." You could tell he had more to say, so she stayed quiet hoping he would continue. "Honey, you know we'd do anything to protect your family. You've gone through a lot."

"Yeah, Dad, I have, but I saw something, or at least I think I saw something and it was bad, Dad."

"Maybe, you think you saw something, honey. Give yourself some more time here and continue to heal; you'll see, things will all come together," smiling now, and reaching for her hand.

Down in the kitchen, another similar conversation was being exchanged. "Do you think she's going to understand?" her brother asked. The kids came meandering in. "What's up guys?" He gave each of them a slap high five. Each was carrying a large five-gallon bucket with white powder. He helped them lift them onto the counter. Momma C handed him some empty kitchen canisters with seals. "Can you put these away while we're out?" not really asking her son.

"Momma C, are you ready?" the two children prodded, heading out the door, clearly ready for their next assignment.

"Right behind you," she responded, leaving her son in the kitchen. At the doorway, she looked back and reassured him, "Don't worry." The kids piled into the truck, taking up their favorite spots. By this time, the dogs rode along too.

They headed down the long drive and turned left out onto the highway, picking up speed toward town. Because they arrived so early, there was plenty of parking with a few straggler metal carts in the parking lot. They left the dogs in the truck with the windows down for air. While walking toward the front doors, she handed them a list of supplies with instructions to meet up at the counter making the best strategy on time. When they entered the foyer of the department store, there were the obvious pictures of the missing children. Momma C looked down and reached into her pocket, giving each grandchild a red pen. And, without hesitation, the children zeroed in on the latest black and white prints and scratched a red X mark against two of the faces. Returning to her side, they proceeded to hand her back the pens, which she just waved off, "No, these are yours now. We've got to go, I've got a hunch and need to check something out."

It was such a relief when Momma C found what she did. The wave of relief was overwhelming; yet at the same time, he cried when Momma C told him what she found. It felt like forever, and it felt good to let it all out. Momma C had found the pasture and the moss field. She had this true detective radar in her genes. Momma C came back to the farm, dropping the children off and calling out to her son to climb in. The drive was not as long as he had thought. He wondered how she had found the trail, but it opened up as they continued to walk, brushing back limbs and entering a clearing. He could see the allure of it all. In the middle of the lush green blanket were three small trees. And then he knew. She stood behind, watching him grieve and waited until he was ready to leave. It was a quiet ride back to the farm. Absently, he fiddled with his own chain, shaking his head, knowing his wife and children were gone, but understanding the balance. He wondered what had happened to their pendants. He kept rethinking that maybe that kid from high school stole them, but then he was missing too.

Not being able to shake off her curiosity which was getting the best of her, Maggie wondered into their mother's room. Neat, orderly, French provincial overstuffed classic chairs and lamps made the room so inviting and comfortable. She noted the layers of differing sized pictures on her mantel and coffee table near the window. Large velvet green drapes hung from the top of the ceiling to puddling on the floor; Mom always went for the more dramatic 'gone with the wind' look. This made her smile. Her mother's jewelry box, given by her mother's mother, was on the dresser. Absently, she walked over and lifted the lid, expecting to see an array of pieces collected over the years. She flipped it wide open and let the top fall back, as what she saw caused her to freeze, standing there trembling. Inside were several, well, more than several, black raisin-shaped pendants. The entire box was full, and the two on top were sticky. She picked one of them up and examined her fingers when the color came off, which of course, at this point, you know was red. There was that smell. The old decay of blood. She dropped the pendant and ran downstairs looking for her brother. She must have screamed because he came running from another direction but toward her.

His first thought as he caught his sister's arms and she collapsed into them was *she knows now*.

Later that evening, after the sedative had taken effect, Momma C came to Maggie's room. "Good, you're awake. We need to talk." Maggie remained quiet, still a bit groggy, but very aware of her fears. "Maggie," her mom started, "we find ways to protect our families, the ones we love. Sometimes we find we can't do it by ourselves or even rely on the systems we have in place. You've not been part of this path; it's not for you and others have been chosen. You are going to have to understand and be a part, much like your father. He's not chosen and you, like him, are not as well."

Maggie sat up, but her head started spinning a bit and she lay back, adjusting her pillow; she needed to sit up to hear better. "What do you mean, be chosen? Who is chosen?"

Her brother tapped on the door. "I saw the light, is she up?" he inquired, walking in.

"Yes, she's up," Momma C said without turning or getting up from the corner of the bed.

Maggie propped her head, and from the side table's low lamp, she got an angle of her brother's neck and noticed for the first time a silver chain she had never really observed before. "The pendants," she said.

"Yes, the pendants," her mother confirmed.

"You kill people for the pendants?" she asked.

"No, I keep things in balance, dear. That's my role," she tried to reassure her.

Full Circle

What happened to Maggie, you ask? She stayed around and she stayed quiet. She had to. The mother of the chosen has to protect her children. Just like her mother did, and her mother's mother. Her brother? He stayed for a while and then moved on to the next town. The case of his family remained open, but he was able to start work again, and for him, that was good enough. The grandfather? He too is getting on – still surviving and will continue to live long, as he keeps supplied with the formula Momma C gives him. The children? Ah, yes, the children had become quite skilled in breaking and grinding down the bones. Clearly, a work of art and they had learned well. No one could imagine the healing properties behind the grains of the white mill. Or the blood. Hard to believe that every juicy bite is an extension of nature keeping the balance. People from all over the world buy and consume truckloads after truckloads of strawberries. You could see how the consumer admires the plumpness, and the deep dark red color; if only they knew the real work that went behind it all. Lastly, Momma C plowed another few acreages for more rows of strawberries and hired more hands. It seemed to be continuing to grow. Last Christmas, I heard the children gave their grandmother another beautiful shiny jewelry box, wasn't that sweet? Remember, you've been warned.